One morning, Inky, Snake, and Bee had seen such a lot of cartoons that they were getting restless.

“I am bored,” said Snake, stretching. “Let’s do something else.”

“Like what?” said Inky and Bee, looking up.

Snake shrugged.

"What about hide and seek?" he said.

"No," said Inky and Bee. "You win every time!"

"What about Monopoly?" said Inky.

"No," said Snake. "I am sick of sitting down."

“What about a game of ‘What’s in the box?’” said Phonic, from his corner.

Inky, Bee, and Snake listened while Phonic explained the rules. “You have a box,” he said, “and you go and collect things to fill it with. All the things must fit in the box. Then we see what everyone has found.”

“I like the sound of that!” said Snake, and Inky and Bee agreed with him. So Inky found three empty boxes and off they all went. Inky and Snake rushed off to the shed and Bee zoomed outside, where she buzzed around in a panic.

“What will go into my box? What will go into my box?” she kept buzzing.

Back at the mouse hole, Phonic found himself alone.

"What can I do while I am waiting?" he brooded. Then he smiled. His screen went blank and then filled up with lots of little green and red ships, which floated across it. Phonic liked this game!

"Bip, bip, ping... kersplat!" A little green ship went up in flames.

"Got you!" muttered Phonic.

Outside, Inky looked around. Then she looked down at her box. It seemed very small indeed. She looked around again.

"Perfect!" she exclaimed as she picked something off the ground.

Just then, Bee zipped by.

"What shall I get? What shall I get?" she was still buzzing, frantically.

Snake was looking around too. He scratched his head.

"Perfect!" he exclaimed, picking something up.

Just then, Bee whizzed by again.

"What will fit? What will fit?" she buzzed.

Snake slithered back to the shed.

"There must be something in here that will fit in my box," he hissed. "Yesss!" he hissed happily, picking up something else and slipping it into his box.

Just then, Bee rushed by again.

"What shall I get? What shall I get?" she buzzed.

Inky was still in the garden. She tried looking under a tree, where she soon found something. She picked it up and tucked it into her box.

"Good," she said to herself. "Where shall I go next?"

Just then, Bee came speeding by.

"What will fit? What shall I get?" she buzzed.

Bee was still frantically hunting for things to go in her box.

"Help!" she was muttering, when suddenly she spotted a feather. "Yes!" she exclaimed. "That will just fit in my box."

She swooped down to pick the feather up.

Inky shut her box.

"That's it!" she said. "I have finished." She looked around. Snake was sitting next to his box, sunning himself. "Have you finished?" called Inky.

"Yes," said Snake, sitting up. They looked around.

"Where is Bee?" said Inky. They looked and looked but Bee was nowhere about.

“Where can she be?” said Snake. He and Inky looked everywhere, but Bee was still nowhere to be found. “Perhaps she has finished too,” said Snake. “Let’s see if she is back with Phonic.”

Back at the mouse hole, they found Bee’s box on the desk, but Bee herself was not there.

“Phonic!” called Inky.

“Er... here I am,” said Phonic, who quickly hid his game and popped back onto the screen.

"Have you seen Bee?" said Snake.

"No, sorry, I was just... er... checking this game," he confessed. "Is that her box there?" Snake and Inky nodded.

"Yes," they agreed, "but we cannot see Bee. We have looked and looked."

"Well, we had better start without her." said Phonic, "but perhaps she will come back soon. She cannot have gone far."

“Come on then,” he continued. “Let’s see what you collected in your boxes.” Inky had found a stamp that someone had dropped by the shed. Next she took out a striped seed, a bit of green string, some sand from the sand box, and a small stone with a hole in it.

“Good job, Inky!” cried Snake and Phonic.

Snake started to take the things out of his box. There was a rubber band, a nail from the shed, a twig, some red wool, and a doll's boot that had been dropped on the ground outside.

"Good job, Snake!" exclaimed Inky and Phonic.

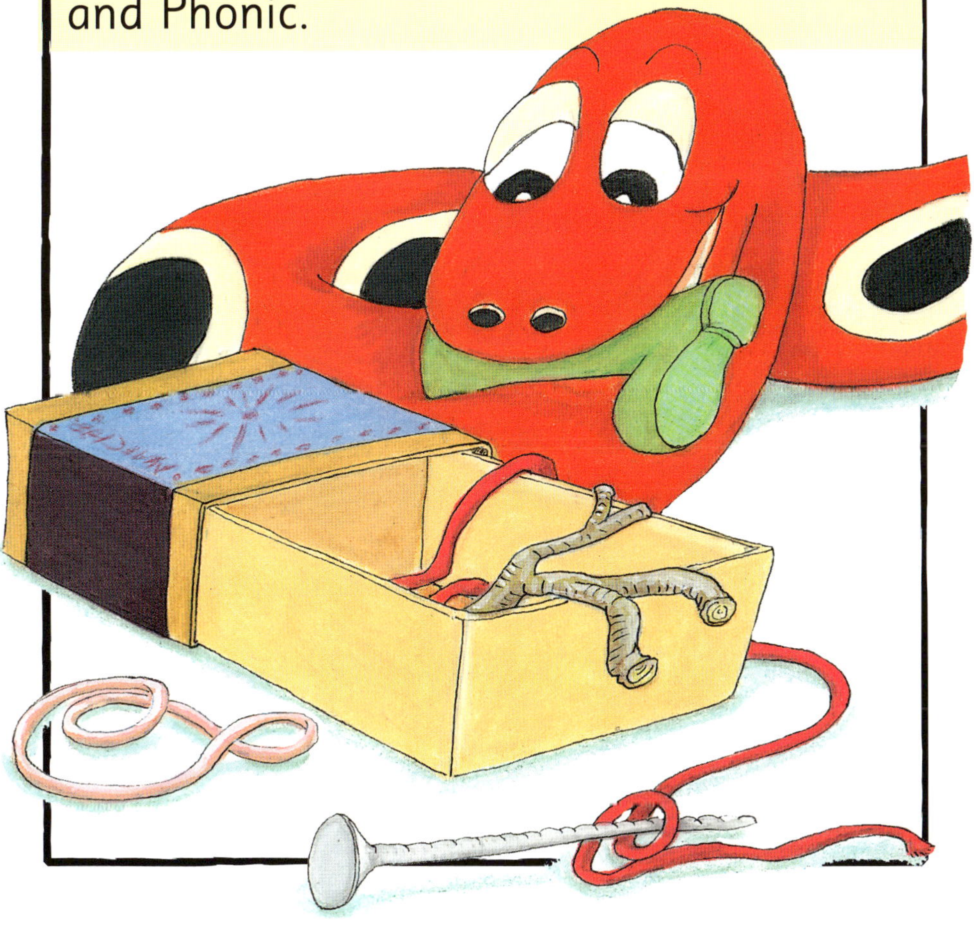

They looked around but Bee was still nowhere to be seen.

"Where can she be?" said Inky.

"Well, let's see what she collected," said Phonic.

Inky scampered up to Bee's box. She tried to see what was inside it, but the box was too heavy for her. Snake slithered up to help. Together they slid the top of the box off, and there inside it was Bee, sound asleep on the feather!

"All that buzzing around looking for things must have worn her out," smiled Inky.